Abigail Adams
CHAMPION FOR WOMEN

BY TYLER OMOTH

Published by The Child's World®
1980 Lookout Drive • Mankato, MN 56003-1705
800-599-READ • www.childsworld.com

Photographs ©: Everett Historical/Shutterstock Images, cover, 1; Everett Collection/Newscom, 5; iStockphoto, 6, 16; North Wind Picture Archives, 8, 15; Victorian Traditions/Shutterstock Images, 10; Joseph Sohm/Shutterstock Images, 12; Everett-Art/Shutterstock Images, 19; Elise Amendola/AP Images, 20

Copyright © 2018 by The Child's World®
All rights reserved. No part of this book may be reproduced or utilized in any form or by any means without written permission from the publisher.

ISBN 9781503823921
LCCN 2017944768

Printed in the United States of America
PA02362

ABOUT THE AUTHOR

Tyler Omoth has written more than 30 books for kids, covering a wide variety of topics. He has also published poetry and award-winning short stories. He loves sports and new adventures. Tyler currently lives in sunny Brandon, Florida, with his wife, Mary.

TABLE OF CONTENTS

Fast Facts 4

Chapter 1
The Second First Lady 7

Chapter 2
Defender of Women's Rights 11

Chapter 3
Mrs. President 17

Think About It 21
Glossary 22
Source Notes 23
To Learn More 24
Index 24

FAST FACTS

Full name
- Abigail Smith Adams

Birthdate
- November 11, 1744, in Weymouth, Massachusetts

Husband
- President John Adams

Children
- Abigail, John Quincy, Susanna, Charles, and Thomas

Years in the White House
- 1797–1801

Accomplishments
- Served as a supporter and unofficial adviser to her husband before and during the time her husband was president of the United States.
- Was a champion of equal education for girls.

- Spoke out against the institution of slavery.
- Against the wishes of her neighbors, helped a black youth in her area get a **formal** education.

Chapter 1

THE SECOND FIRST LADY

Abigail Adams sat in a dimly lit room in her home in Quincy, Massachusetts. She was wearing a basic housedress. The tan color displayed the wear and tear of daily life for a woman in 1797. She reached out her hand to take the trembling hand of the elderly woman before her. The woman was her mother-in-law, Susanna Boylston Adams Hall, and she was dying. Abigail's husband, John, was in Philadelphia while Abigail tended to his mother. He was accepting his election as the second president of the United States of America. This made Abigail the second First Lady of a brand-new nation. From this day forward, she knew their lives would be changed forever.

◄ Abigail Adams became First Lady on March 4, 1797.

▲ Girls of Abigail's time were typically not allowed to go to school. Instead, they learned to keep a household.

Abigail was born in 1744 in Weymouth, Massachusetts. At that time, most girls did not receive a formal education. Abigail did not attend school. But her parents still encouraged her to learn to read and write.

One night, Abigail put on her favorite dress and went into town for a social event. She was 17 years old.

A young man named John Adams noticed her. The two talked and connected over their mutual love of reading.

Three years later, John and Abigail were married. Abigail loved John's personality. He was a lawyer, and she constantly **debated** with him. Soon, Abigail became John's most trusted adviser on all topics.

In the 1760s, Britain ruled over the American colonies. As he worked as a lawyer, John also had worked to build the **revolution** against England. Now, he was about to be sworn in as the president of a newly freed nation.

Abigail sat holding her mother-in-law's hand in the dark. She knew that her husband would need her now more than ever.

> "Learning is not attained by chance, it must be sought for with ardour and attended to with diligence."[1]
>
> —*Abigail Adams*

Chapter 2

DEFENDER OF WOMEN'S RIGHTS

It was March 1776. Abigail sat at her desk at home. The spring sunlight shone through the window. Her young daughter played happily on the floor behind her. Abigail sharpened a quill. She dipped the tip into her pot of black ink. John was in Philadelphia with the **Continental Congress**. She wrote to him with some advice.

I long to hear that you have declared an independency. And, by the way, in the new code of laws which I suppose it will be necessary for you to make, I desire you would remember the ladies and be more generous and favorable to them than your ancestors. Do not put such unlimited power into the hands of the husbands.

◄ John Adams (center), along with other founding fathers, helped create the government of the United States.

▲ Abigail had a large impact on raising awareness of women's lack of rights in the 1700s. A statue of her and her son John Quincy stands in Quincy, Massachusetts.

Remember, all men would be tyrants if they could. If particular care and attention is not paid to the ladies, we are determined to **foment** *a rebellion, and will not hold ourselves bound by any laws in which we have no voice or representation.[2]*

Abigail knew that she had been lucky. She lived in a time when most girls did not receive any formal education. Yet, her family had supported her desires to read and learn. However, as an adult, Abigail still lived in a time period when women had few rights. Abigail had no voting powers. She could not hold political office. She even had very few rights to own property.

> "If we mean to have heroes, statesmen, and philosophers, we should have learned [educated] women."[3]
>
> —Abigail Adams

Abigail wrote more letters to her husband. And she wrote them to anyone who would read about her ideas on the education of women. Abigail believed that young boys needed to grow into responsible adults. They were to be leaders of the nation. In order for this to happen, the women who raised them needed to be educated as well. Abigail knew that women were more than caretakers.

Women not only raised children but often handled their husbands' **finances** as well. Some women even had jobs while their husbands were away.

Abigail joined forces with other early **feminists**, such as writer Judith Sargent Murray. These women worked to create a movement toward equal rights. Abigail wanted to create a system for the education of women. She believed in equal rights in voting and property. Abigail also wanted to see slaves freed. She believed that freedom and education were not meant for a select few. Abigail spoke out on these issues. She often tried to use John's power to create change.

Women in New Jersey could vote in 1776. It took another 144 years for women in all states to be able to have this same right.

Chapter 3

MRS. PRESIDENT

Abigail stepped off a ship and onto dry land for the first time in more than five weeks. It was 1784. Abigail's legs wobbled a bit as she got used to the sudden lack of motion. She wore her finest dress, which had been carefully packed away for the trip. Finally, she was in France. John had been here for a diplomatic mission. They had been apart for nearly five years.

Throughout their marriage, John and Abigail Adams exchanged many letters. These were more than just letters of affection and news of the day. They were letters between two **confidants**.

◀ Abigail was often separated from John. They agreed that it was okay because he was helping build a new nation.

They trusted each other. John sought out Abigail's advice on many political matters. He valued her opinion greatly.

When John was **inaugurated** in 1797, Abigail's status with her husband did not change. She continued to advise him on many matters. Some other officials resented her position. They began to refer to her as Mrs. President. They wanted to imply that she made more decisions than her husband.

Abigail did not always tell John what he wanted to hear. But she always gave her honest opinion. From 1798 to 1800 John had to deal with the XYZ Affair. This was a disagreement with France that threatened to become a war. John wished for a peaceful resolution. But Abigail disagreed with him. She thought the United States should declare war on France. However, the countries stayed at peace.

Abigail continued to speak up for women's rights until her death in October 1818.

▲ Some of John and Abigail's letters have been compiled into a book called *My Dearest Friend.*

However, Abigail did not always disagree with her husband. There were many times when the two agreed. Whether Abigail agreed or disagreed with her husband, John always respected her opinion. He always wanted to know what Abigail thought about an issue.

As the second First Lady, Abigail Adams proved that the position could involve much more than just being the president's wife. Abigail was a powerful force in the political world of the late 1700s.

THINK ABOUT IT

- Abigail Adams believed that to be able to raise intelligent children, women needed to be better-educated themselves. Do you think it is important for everyone to have the same opportunities for education? Why or why not?
- Abigail Adams read everything she could find when she was young. How do you think reading helps educate?
- While he was a diplomat and president, John Adams asked for advice from his wife. In a time when women's opinions were not considered equal to men's, why do you think John did this?
- In her letter to John in March 1776, Abigail said that if women were granted no power, they would eventually start "a rebellion." Why do you think it was important for women to be able to vote?

GLOSSARY

confidant (KON-fi-dahnt): A confidant is a person with whom one shares secrets and personal thoughts. John Adams considered Abigail Adams his greatest confidant.

Continental Congress (kon-tuh-NEN-tull KONG-gris): The Continental Congress was a gathering of representatives from the 13 colonies that formed the government of the United States. Abigail wrote letters to John while he attended the Continental Congress.

debated (deh-BAY-ted): To have debated something is to have discussed a topic from opposing viewpoints. Abigail debated with John on many issues.

feminists (FEM-uh-nists): Feminists are people who believe that women are equal to men and should receive the same rights. Abigail joined many feminists to fight for women's right to vote.

finances (FY-nan-sez): Finances is the management of personal or business money. Abigail handled the family finances while John was in France.

foment (foh-MENT): To foment is to instigate or stir up. Abigail promised to foment a rebellion if women's education rights were not considered by men.

formal (FOR-muhl): To be formal is to be official or publicly recognized. Abigail did not receive a formal education.

inaugurated (in-AW-gyuh-ray-ted): When someone is inaugurated, he or she is formally admitted into public office. John was inaugurated as the second president of the United States.

revolution (rev-uh-LOO-shuhn): A revolution is a violent takeover of a country's current government by the people living there. John worked on the revolution against Britain.

SOURCE NOTES

1. "Abigail Adams to John Quincy Adams." *Massachusetts Historical Society*. Massachusetts Historical Society, n.d. Web. 9 June 2017.

2. "Abigail Adams Urges Husband to 'Remember the Ladies.'" *History.com*. A&E Television Networks, n.d. Web. 9 June 2017.

3. "Abigail Adams to John Adams." *Massachusetts Historical Society*. Massachusetts Historical Society, n.d. Web. 9 June 2017.

TO LEARN MORE

Books

Krull, Kathleen. *A Kids' Guide to America's First Ladies.* New York, NY: HarperCollins, 2017.

Maloof, Torrey. *Abigail Adams and the Women Who Shaped America.* Huntington Beach, CA: Teacher Created Materials Inc., 2016.

Wells, Peggy Sue. *Abigail Adams.* Kennett Square, PA: Purple Toad Publishing, 2016.

Web Sites

Visit our Web site for links about Abigail Adams: childsworld.com/links

Note to Parents, Teachers, and Librarians: We routinely verify our Web links to make sure they are safe and active sites. So encourage your readers to check them out!

INDEX

Adams, John, 7, 9, 11, 14, 17, 18, 20

Britain, 9

Continental Congress, 11

education, 8, 13, 14

equal rights, 14

feminists, 14

France, 17, 18

Hall, Susanna Boylston Adams, 7

letters, 13, 17

Mrs. President, 18

Murray, Judith Sargent, 14

Philadelphia, Pennsylvania, 7, 11

Weymouth, Massachusetts, 8

women, 11–14

XYZ Affair, 18